Angelina Ballerina™
by the Sea

T0371155

Based on the stories by Katharine Holabird
Based on the illustrations by Helen Craig

Simon Spotlight
New York   London   Toronto   Sydney   New Delhi
An imprint of Simon & Schuster Children's Publishing Division
1230 Avenue of the Americas, New York, New York 10020 • This Simon Spotlight edition May 2022
© 2022 Helen Craig Ltd. and Katharine Holabird. The Angelina Ballerina name and character and the dancing Angelina logo are trademarks of HIT Entertainment Limited, Katharine Holabird, and Helen Craig. • All rights reserved, including the right of reproduction in whole or in part in any form.
SIMON SPOTLIGHT and colophon are registered trademarks of Simon & Schuster, Inc.
For information about special discounts for bulk purchases, please contact Simon & Schuster Special Sales
at 1–866-506-1949 or business@simonandschuster.com. • Manufactured in the United States of America 0523 LAK
2 3 4 5 6 7 8 9 10 • ISBN 978-1-6659-1392-8 • ISBN 978-1-6659-1393-5 (ebook)

Angelina Ballerina woke up on a bright, sunny morning with a big smile. Today she was going to the seaside with her family and her best friend, Alice! She could already tell that it was going to be a wonderful day.

Angelina leapt out of bed and changed into her swimsuit. She helped her sister Polly get dressed too. Then they packed their bags with everything they needed for the beach, like hats, towels, and plenty of toys to play in the sand.

"I can't wait to build a beautiful sandcastle with Alice," Angelina said.

In the kitchen, Mr. and Mrs. Mouseling were busy packing a picnic basket full of treats.

"Good morning, girls," their mother said. "There are cheddar scones and milk on the table for breakfast. As soon as Henry and Alice arrive, we'll be ready to leave for the seaside."

A few minutes later, the doorbell rang. "I'll get it!" Angelina cried happily. She ran to the door and opened it. It was her cousin Henry and Alice!

"I can't wait for us to go to the seaside!" Alice exclaimed. "We are going to have the very best time."

A short time later, Angelina, her family, and Alice arrived at the seaside.

Angelina's parents put down the beach blanket, set up the umbrella, and gave Polly and Henry a bag of toys to play with.

"Catch, Polly!" Henry cheered as he tossed a beach ball into the air.

"What should we do first?" Angelina asked Alice.
"Let's make sandcastles!" Alice suggested. "That's my favorite thing to do at the beach!"

Alice fetched seawater with a pail, and Angelina scooped up sand with her shovel. Then they happily worked together, making a beautiful big sandcastle with the wet sand.

Angelina carved a window out of the tallest sand tower. "I would like to live in this room," she said. "Every morning, I could gaze outside at the sea!"

Alice carved a window right next to Angelina's. "This will be my room!" she said.

Angelina and Alice decided to walk along the shore and look for seashells to decorate their sandcastle. They found a perfectly smooth one, a shiny pink one, and even a spiky one!

Alice picked up a conch and held the opening to her ear. "You can hear the ocean waves!" she said, handing it over to Angelina.

Angelina listened closely. Alice was right—it sounded like a whole ocean was inside the shell!

The two friends returned to their sandcastle with their bucket of seashells. Once they finished decorating, everyone came by to admire their work. Henry thought the sandcastle looked just like the Royal Palace!

Angelina and Alice beamed.

After eating sandwiches and resting their tummies, Angelina and Alice decided to play in the water.

"Jump!" Angelina exclaimed, pointing to a wave.

Alice giggled as the waves tickled her toes. "I love splashing in the sea!" she said.

After they jumped in the waves, Angelina suggested they do some ballet routines together.

"Miss Lilly will be so proud that we practiced dancing while we were at the seaside," Angelina told Alice.

Angelina and Alice began twirling across the sand. Then Angelina tried doing a very high leap, and she accidentally landed right on top of the sandcastle!

"Oh no!" Alice cried.

"Oops!" said Angelina. "I'm really sorry."

"We had worked so hard on it," Alice said, sniffling.

"How about we fly our kite?" Angelina suggested. "Or go for a walk along the shore?"

Alice shook her head and buried her face in her hands.

Angelina was worried about Alice being so upset. She remembered that Alice had said building sandcastles was her favorite thing to do at the beach. Even if the ruined sandcastle didn't bother Angelina, it clearly mattered to her friend.

Angelina looked at their seashells, now scattered around in the sand. Then she thought of a surprise to cheer up Alice.

A little while later, Angelina walked over to Alice. "I'm sorry about the sandcastle," Angelina said. "I made something for you, and I hope you like it." She gave Alice a bracelet made out of the seashells they had collected together.

Alice put on the bracelet and smiled at Angelina. "Thank you," she said. "I know it was just an accident. I want to build another sandcastle, but can we have ice cream first?"

"Yes!" Angelina laughed, and the two best friends skipped to the ice cream stand, hand in hand.